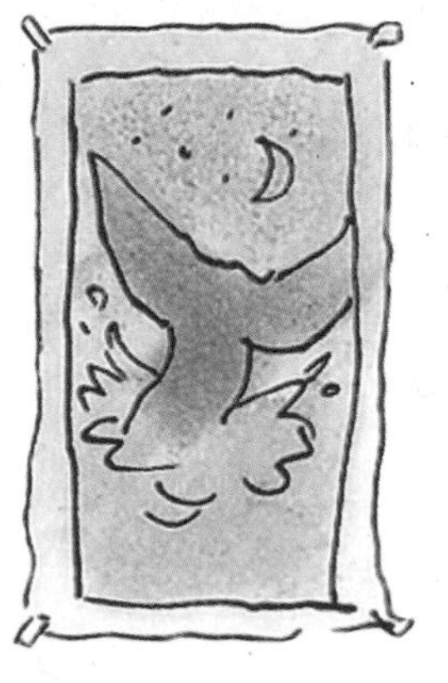

SIMON JAMES often writes about a child's relationship with the natural world and never with more poignancy than here in *Dear Greenpeace*; the story of a young girl called Emily who finds a whale in her pond. Warm-hearted and thoughtful, this is an enchanting ecological tale that remains as important a book today as the day it was created, and is a call to action for us all.

ABOUT DEAR GREENPEACE, Simon says, "If this book has encouraged children to write letters highlighting their concerns about wildlife – or anything else they feel strongly about – then that can only be a good thing. I feel the plight of the natural world is an issue which needs the voices of the young." He adds, "This book is also a celebration of imagination and creativity. Does Emily *really* have a whale in her pond? Only Emily knows."

To David and to Lucy
with love

The correspondence in this book is a work of fiction.
The name Greenpeace is used by kind permission of
Greenpeace UK, Canonbury Villas, London N1 2PN

First published 1991 by Walker Books Ltd
87 Vauxhall Walk, London SE11 5HJ

This edition published 2016

2 4 6 8 10 9 7 5 3 1

This book has been typeset in Palatino
and handlettered by Simon James

Printed in China

British Library Cataloguing in Publication Data:
a catalogue record for this book is available from the British Library

ISBN 978-1-4063-6740-9

www.walker.co.uk
www.simonjamesbooks.com

SIMON JAMES

Dear Greenpeace

WALKER BOOKS
AND SUBSIDIARIES
LONDON • BOSTON • SYDNEY • AUCKLAND

Dear Greenpeace,

I love whales very much and I think I saw one in my pond today. Please send me some information on whales, as I think he might be hurt.

Love
Emily

Dear Emily,

Here are some details about whales. I don't think you'll find it was a whale you saw, because whales don't live in ponds, but in salt water.

Yours sincerely,

Greenpeace

Dear Greenpeace,

I am now putting salt into the pond every day before school and last night I saw my whale smile. I think he is feeling better. Do you think he might be lost?

Love
Emily

2

Dear Emily,

Please don't put any more salt in the pond, I'm sure your parents won't be pleased.

I'm afraid there can't be a whale in your pond, because whales don't get lost, they always know where they are in the oceans.

Yours sincerely,

Greenpeace

Dear Greenpeace,

Tonight I am very happy because I saw my whale jump up and spurt lots of water. He looked blue.

Does this mean he might be a blue whale?

Love

Emily

P.S. What can I feed him with?

Dear Emily,

Blue whales are blue and they eat tiny shrimp-like creatures that live in the sea. However I must tell you that a blue whale is much too big to live in your pond.

Yours sincerely,

Greenpeace

P.S. Perhaps it is a blue goldfish?

goldfish

Dear Greenpeace,

Last night I read your letter to my whale. Afterwards he let me stroke his head. It was very exciting.

I secretly took him some crunched-up cornflakes and bread-crumbs. This morning I looked in the pond and they were all gone!

I think I shall call him Arthur, what do you think?

Love

Emily

Dear Emily,

I must point out to you quite forcefully now that in no way could a whale live in your pond. You may not know that whales are migratory, which means they travel great distances each day.

I am sorry to disappoint you.

Yours sincerely,

Greenpeace

Dear Greenpeace,

Tonight I'm a little sad. Arthur has gone. I think your letter made sense to him and he has decided to be migratory again.

Love

Emily

Dear Emily,

Please don't be too sad, it really was impossible for a whale to live in your pond. Perhaps when you are older you would like to sail the oceans studying and protecting whales with us.

Yours sincerely,

Greenpeace

Dear Greenpeace,

It's been the happiest day!
I went to the seaside and you'll
never guess, but I saw Arthur!
I called to him and he smiled.
I knew it was Arthur because
he let me stroke his head.

I gave him some of my
sandwich...

and then we said goodbye.
I shouted that I loved him very much and, I hope you don't mind, I said you loved him too.

love
Emily (and Arthur)

The End

SIMON JAMES is one of the UK's leading author–illustrators. He has won the Smarties Book Prize, for *Leon and Bob*, and been shortlisted for the prestigious Kate Greenaway Medal, for *Days Like This*. He has won numerous awards for *Baby Brains*, including the Red House Children's Book Award. He is a regular speaker in schools and at festivals across the UK and the US. To find out more about Simon James and his books, visit www.simonjamesbooks.com

Other books by Simon James

ISBN 978-1-4063-3842-3

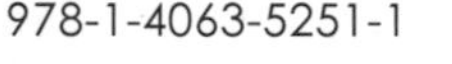

ISBN 978-1-4063-5251-1

ISBN 978-1-4063-6053-0

ISBN 978-1-4063-0849-5

ISBN 978-1-84428-522-8

ISBN 978-1-4063-0846-4

ISBN 978-1-84428-467-2